HURRICANE GUEST

Mike and Tess made special plans for entertaining their English houseguest, Peter, on his first visit to America. But the plans were forgotten in the excitement created by another surprise visitor—a hurricane.

HURRICANE GUEST

by Sam and Beryl Epstein

illustrated by Marilyn Miller

Random House
New York

CONTENTS

HURRICANE GUEST

Be Our Guest

Mike and Tess Davis and their mother moved to the summer cottage the Saturday after school closed. Mr. Davis came along for the weekend. His own vacation wouldn't begin until late August.

They bought the rowboat that very day. She was fresh-painted, even if she wasn't brand new. She was white, with green trim. Mike and Tess thought she was the most beautiful boat they had ever seen.

Mrs. Davis said, "Let's name her the *Em-Tee*. The *Em* will stand for M, for Mike. The *Tee* will be T, for Tess."

Mr. Davis painted the new name on her hull right away. Then Mike and Tess were prouder of her than

ever.

"Come on," Mr. Davis said. "Let's take her out for a row. There's room for all of us."

They piled in. Mr. Davis took the oars. He rowed to the head of Duck Creek, and back to their dock.

"Whew!" he said. "That's hard work. I hope by next year we'll be able to get a motor for her."

Later Mike and Tess took the *Em-Tee* out alone.

Mike rowed easily up-creek with the tide. But rowing back took all his strength.

"I sure wish we didn't have to wait a whole year for a motor," he said.

"I have an idea," Tess said. "You and I could earn money and buy one!"

"You're crazy," Mike told her. "Even a second-hand motor would cost at least fifty dollars."

"But you don't collect stamps any more," Tess said. "You could sell your stamp collection. And that would give us a good start on a motor fund."

"Yes," Mike said slowly. "I guess it would."

"And lots of boats come in to the town wharf," Tess went on. "You're good with boats. You could help people cast off, and tie up. And they'd pay you."

"Yes," Mike said slowly again. "Maybe they would."

"And I could earn money too," Tess said. "There's a new family in the gray cottage. Their name is Correll. And they've got twins—Jim and Jody—who are four years old. I'm sure Mrs. Correll would let me help her take care of them."

Mike sat and thought for a while.

Then he said, "Well, it would certainly be great if we could do it. Especially if we could earn a motor by the third week in August. You know—when Dad's vacation begins."

"That would be terrific!" Tess said. "Let's try! But let's not tell Dad and Mother. Then we can give them a wonderful surprise."

Mr. Davis went back to the city on Monday morning.

Right after he left, Mike went to see a boy he knew who collected stamps. The boy looked at Mike's collection for a long time. Then he offered Mike $5.25 for it.

"It's a pretty good beginning for our fund," Mike told Tess. "And I'll go to the town wharf this afternoon. Maybe I'll earn some more."

Tess had news too. "Mrs. Correll is going to pay me a quarter for looking after the boys this afternoon!"

"Great!" Mike said.

5

"Oh, and Mike," Tess went on. "I have an idea that might help you. Just listen when I say the name of our boat."

She took a deep breath. Then she said, *"Em-Tee. Em-Tee. Em-Tee.* There! What does it sound like, when I say it fast like that?"

"It sounds like *Em-Tee,"* Mike said.

"But listen, Mike," Tess said. *"Em-Tee!* There! Doesn't that sound like *Empty?"*

"Well, yes. Sort of," Mike said. "So what?"

"Well, you know people always ask what a boat's name means," Tess said. "So when they ask you, you could explain first about the M and T, for us. Then you could say it also stands for Empty. Empty-because-she-doesn't-have-a-motor-in-her. And that will give you a chance to say we're trying to earn money. So maybe they'd pay you more."

Mike looked at her. "You certainly get a lot of ideas," he said. "But I guess I could try it," he added.

Almost before they knew it, the 4th of July had come and gone. Then it was the middle of July. It was being a wonderful summer. Except for the motor fund. On July 15 all they had saved was $13.90.

The next afternoon Tess sat on the dock waiting for Mike to come home.

"At this rate," she thought, "we'll never earn a motor."

She tried to cheer herself up by thinking about the twins. They were so funny! And so smart!

That day she'd said, "Let's pretend to be butterflies." She expected them to wave their arms around, like

6

wings. Instead Jody got down on his stomach, and wriggled.

"I have to be a caterpillar first," he explained. "Everybody is a caterpillar before he is a butterfly."

Tess saw Mike coming. She wanted to tell him about Jody. But she knew she had to tell him something else first. She had to tell him she wouldn't earn her usual quarter the next day. Mrs. Correll was taking the twins away for the afternoon.

Mike pulled up alongside the dock.

"Ye little hermit crabs!" he said. That was the expression he had invented to use when he was really disgusted. "I only earned a dime all afternoon!"

"Oh, dear!" Tess said. "And I won't earn anything at all tomorrow. The twins aren't going to be here."

"Tess! Mike!" Mrs. Davis had just stepped out of the car. She was waving a letter.

"It must be from Daddy," Tess said. "Come on!"

Mrs. Davis was putting groceries away when they reached the house. An air-mail letter lay on the table.

"But Daddy doesn't write air-mail letters," Tess said.

"No." Mrs. Davis was smiling. "That letter is from Mr. Blake, father of Peter Blake."

"Peter Blake." Mike said the name over to himself. "That was the name of the pen pal I wrote to last year. The boy in England."

"Exactly!" Mrs. Davis said. "This letter is from his father. Mr. Blake is coming over here on business, and Peter is coming too. His father asks if we'd like to have Peter visit us for a few days. Wouldn't that be nice?"

Mike thought about it for a minute. "But Peter and

I were pen pals because we were both collecting stamps," Mike said finally. "And I don't collect any more. So what could we talk about? Besides, we're terribly busy, Mom. I guess you'd better tell him no."

"My! What a hospitable speech!" Mrs. Davis raised her eyebrows at Mike. "Suppose you read the letter first. Then perhaps you'll be able to say something more polite."

Mike and Tess took the letter into the living room. They read it together.

The surprising part of the letter said: "But Peter has given up collecting stamps. So he is afraid that he and Mike might not have anything to talk about."

"Oh!" Mike said. "But we still don't have time to have company, do we?" he asked Tess. "We have to keep working, if we—"

Tess interrupted him. "Mike! Look!" She was pointing to the top of the letter.

Mr. Blake had written on his office paper. The words printed at the top said: BLAKE MARINE ENGINES.

"Aren't marine engines the same as boat motors?" Tess asked.

"Sure," Mike said.

"Then don't you see?" Tess demanded. "It's an absolutely terrific coincidence! Wait till you hear my idea!"

Mike sighed. "Another one?"

"Just listen," Tess told him. "We'll invite Peter to visit us. We'll give him a terrific time. Then his father will want to give us a present. And Peter will tell him we need a motor. So Mr. Blake will give us one!"

Mike stared at her. "You don't go around being nice

9

to people just so you'll get presents."

"But people do give presents when they're guests," Tess said. "We gave Aunt Sally a cook-out grill."

"Sure," Mike said. "But we stayed a week at Aunt Sal's. And there were four of us. Mr. Blake says Peter would only stay a few days. And there's only one of him. Besides, a motor is a lot bigger present than a grill."

"But Mr. Blake makes the motors himself," Tess reminded him. "Probably they don't cost him very much."

"Maybe not," Mike said slowly. "It wouldn't hurt to invite Peter, I guess. Of course, we wouldn't count on anything. We'd go right on earning money—"

"Of course," Tess said quickly.

"It just might be worth trying, Tess. It might!" Mike began to grin.

Afterward they told Mrs. Davis that Mike had changed his mind about Peter. And they told her ways they had already thought of for giving Peter a good time.

"We'll have tea every day," Tess said. "I read in a book that English people always drink it."

"And they like Yorkshire pudding," Mike said. "What is that, Mom? Can you make it?"

"Let me ask you something," Mrs. Davis said. "Suppose you visited England—or India or France. Would you want people to feed you hamburgers all the time? Because they had read that Americans like hamburgers?"

"Sure," Mike said. "I could eat hamburgers every day."

"So could I," Tess said. "But I see what Mother means. We ought to show Peter the way we do things. Not give him the same things he has at home."

Her mother smiled. "That's just what I mean, Tess."

"All right," Mike said. "So we'll have a cook-out the very first night. With hamburgers."

Mrs. Davis smiled again. "That's a fine idea," she said. "I'll write to Mr. and Mrs. Blake tonight. And you must write to Peter yourself, Mike."

After dinner Mike borrowed a sheet of his mother's paper. Then he looked around and found a pen. "Dear Peter," he began. The rest of the letter said:

"My sister and I hope you will visit us. We will take you swimming and fishing and crabbing. We will row you around in our boat. We will have to row because she does not have a motor. But we hope you will enjoy yourself. Please be our guest. Your friend, Mike."

Cook-Out,
Cook-In

By the end of July everything was settled.

Peter and his father were going to fly to the United States. They would arrive in New York on the second Wednesday in August. Then Mr. Blake would put his son on a train. Peter would reach Southport at five o'clock. He would stay until Mr. Blake came for him, on Saturday.

The first week of August seemed to go very slowly. The motor fund was only up to $21.15.

"Let's stop worrying," Tess said. "I'm sure my idea will work. What shall we eat at our cook-out?"

14

They talked about it. Then they made a list. It read:

Hamburgers (Ask Peter if he likes his rare, or medium, or well-done.)
Rolls
Sweet pickles
Sour pickles (In case Peter doesn't like sweet ones.)
Potato chips (Barbecue flavored.)
Potato chips (Plain, in case Peter doesn't like barbecue flavor.)
Chocolate cake (Tess will make, from cake mix.)
Raisin cookies (In case Peter doesn't like cake.)
Milk
Lemonade (In case Peter doesn't like milk.)

They showed the list to their mother.

She looked surprised. "It's very thoughtful of you to give Peter so many choices," she said.

"We want to make sure he enjoys himself," Tess said.

"And we'll eat up the leftovers after he's gone," Mike promised. "Even if we have to eat a whole meal of pickles and potato chips."

He and Tess made other lists of food too. One was for the boat picnic they planned for Thursday. One was for the lunch they would take when they went fishing Friday. They planned to have fresh-caught fish Friday night.

"Unless Peter doesn't like fish," Tess said. "If he doesn't, we can have hot dogs."

Finally it was the second Tuesday in August. Tess and Mike went to bed early, to make the next day come sooner.

15

Mike got up first on Wednesday morning. He looked out of the window. "Ye little hermit crabs!" he said.

It was raining.

He banged on Tess's door. "It's raining!" he shouted. He could hear Tess jump out of bed.

"Oh! It is!" she said. "How awful. Let's get a weather report."

They were listening to it when Mrs. Davis joined them.

"Rain has been falling since midnight," the announcer said. "The center of this storm is several hundred miles to the south. Southport is just inside the northern edge of it. At present the storm appears to be moving out to sea. If it continues to move eastward, our weather will clear by tonight. In that case tomorrow will be warm and sunny."

"*If* it continues to move eastward," Tess said. "But suppose it doesn't? What will we do?"

"Now cheer up," Mrs. Davis said. "We don't have to worry yet. And get dressed, both of you. We'll do our shopping right after breakfast."

They ate quickly and drove to the store. They bought hamburger and rolls. They bought potato chips (two kinds), pickles (two kinds), cake mix, and cookies. They bought things for the boat-picnic sandwiches too.

When they got home Tess made the cake. Even Mike said it looked beautiful when it was done.

After lunch Mike chose some of his favorite books for Peter's room. Tess and her mother made Peter's bed.

Then Mike put on a clean pair of slacks and a clean shirt. Tess put on her favorite blue dress.

After that there was nothing more they could do.

"It's three o'clock," Tess said. "Do you think the rain will stop soon, Mother?"

"We'll just have to hope," Mrs. Davis said.

At four o'clock it was still raining.

"We'll have to give up the cook-out," Mrs. Davis said. "Even if it clears soon the grass will be too wet."

"Then everything's ruined!" Tess said. "Everything!"

"Nonsense!" Mrs. Davis said. "We'll have a fire in the fireplace instead. We can cook our hamburgers there. Let's get things ready."

Mike laid the fire. Tess set a table in the living

room. She used her mother's prettiest dishes. She put her cake in the middle.

"It does look nice, doesn't it?" she said. "Maybe Peter will enjoy a cook-in just as much as a cook-out."

At five minutes to five they were at the station. At one minute to five the train came in sight. They got out of the car.

"You take this umbrella for Peter," Mrs. Davis told Mike. "Tess and I will share the other one."

The train stopped. A man got off. Then a woman. Then a boy.

"That must be Peter," Mrs. Davis said.

They walked toward him. He was wearing a cap, a gray jacket and gray shorts. The clothes didn't look at all like the clothes Mike and his friends wore.

"Peter?" Mrs. Davis said. "I'm Mrs. Davis. And this is Tess, and Mike."

"How do you do?" Peter bowed to her and shook hands.

"Ye little hermit crabs!" Mike said to himself. He thought it was silly for a boy to bow.

Then Peter shook hands with Tess and Mike.

Mike thought, "At least he doesn't bow to us."

He and Tess said, "Hello." Peter said, "How do you do?"

Mike and Tess couldn't think of anything else to say. They all walked to the car.

Mrs. Davis backed out of the parking lot. They started home.

"Did the weather make your flight rough, Peter?"

19

Mrs. Davis asked.

"We bounced a couple of times," Peter told her. "But it was wizard."

In the back seat Tess and Mike looked at each other.

"What does wizard mean?" Tess whispered.

"Shh!" Mike said.

"We're so glad you could visit us," Mrs. Davis said.

"So am I," Peter said. "It's wizard."

Mrs. Davis turned into their driveway. They all ran through the rain to the house.

"Mike will show you to your room, Peter," Mrs. Davis said. "You probably want to unpack right away. We'll light the fire in the meantime."

"Thank you," Peter said. "A fire sounds wizard."

Suddenly Tess had the feeling that Peter was homesick.

"We're sorry it's raining," she said. "We wanted to have a cook-out for you. But we'll have a cook-in instead."

"Come on," Mike was saying. He took Peter's bag. Peter followed him across the hall toward the bedrooms.

Mike came back in a minute. In the guest room Peter had said something about being grateful to Mike and Tess for inviting him. The words gave Mike a funny feeling. They made him ashamed, somehow, of their secret hope of getting a motor. But he didn't want to admit it. He pretended to be cross.

"Ye little hermit crabs!" he said. "Can't he say anything but wizard?"

"I think he's trying to be nice," Tess said. "And I think wizard probably means good."

20

"I think so too, Tess," her mother said. "I think he's trying very hard to be nice."

Mike knelt down and lit the fire. It blazed up quickly. The room looked bright and gay. They waited for Peter to come out.

Mike walked up and down. Tess walked around the table.

"Children!" Mrs. Davis said. "Do sit down!"

Mike sat down. He put his hands in his pockets. He took them out again. Tess stared at the fire.

Fifteen minutes ticked away on the clock.

"Ye little hermit crabs!" Mike said. "What's he doing?"

"Why don't you go and see?" Mrs. Davis said. "Perhaps he needs help unpacking."

Mike and Tess went toward the guest room. The door was open just as Mike had left it. They looked inside.

Peter's bag hadn't been opened. Peter was lying on the bed. His cap was still in his hand. He looked as if he had sat down and then fallen backward.

He was fast asleep.

Mike and Tess stared at him. Mrs. Davis joined them.

"Poor boy!" she said. "Of course he was worn out. It's the difference in time."

"The difference in what?" Mike asked.

"Peter left home this morning by English time," Mrs. Davis said. "That's five hours ahead of ours. If he were still at home, it would be after ten now. No wonder he fell asleep—with the excitement of the trip and all."

21

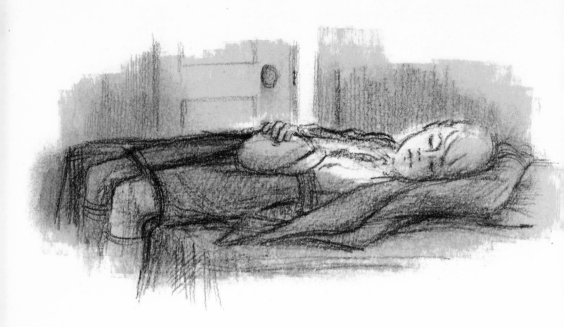

"But what about our cook-in?" Tess asked. She didn't feel so sorry for Peter now. He had no *right* to go to sleep, she thought.

Mike remembered being almost ashamed of hoping to get a motor by being nice to Peter. Now he thought it was Peter who should be ashamed, for going to sleep when he was a guest. "You wake him up, Mom," he said.

"I will do no such thing!" Mrs. Davis said. "The very idea! You want Peter to enjoy himself, don't you?"

"Well—yes," Tess said.

"Yes, but—" Mike said.

"Then we'll let him sleep," their mother said firmly.

Mike looked at Tess. "Ye little hermit crabs!" he said.

Audrey
Came on Thursday

"Mike! Wake up!"

Mike opened his eyes. His mother was bending over him.

"Get dressed," Mrs. Davis said. Then she disappeared.

Mike jumped out of bed. He looked at the clock. It was only six o'clock! In summer his mother never got up until eight. He wondered what had happened.

He pulled on his jeans and a shirt. Then he remembered. Peter Blake had arrived last night! And had fallen asleep, the minute he got in the house.

Mike looked out the window for the first time.

The rain had stopped.

"Maybe Mom just wants us to get ready for the boat

23

picnic," Mike thought.

He and Tess came into the kitchen at the same time. Mrs. Davis didn't wait for them to ask questions.

"A hurricane is heading for Southport," she said.

"A real hurricane?" Tess's sleepy eyes flew wide open.

"Honestly, Mom?" Mike asked.

"Honestly, yes. A real hurricane," Mrs. Davis said.

She was frying a panful of bacon.

"There was a warning on the late news last night," she said. "The storm that was heading out to sea has turned around. And it has grown much worse. It is a real hurricane now. Its official name is Audrey. The early news this morning said it will probably strike here before noon."

"Will Audrey be a bad one, Mom?" Mike asked.

Hurricane Betsy had struck Southport the year before. It had brought strong winds and high tides. Two houses on the ocean beach had been smashed by the waves. Even little Duck Creek had overflowed its banks so far that it covered most of the Davis lawn. It had almost reached the house before the tide turned, and the water fell back.

"They say it will probably be at least as bad as Betsy," Mrs. Davis said. "So we have a lot to do."

"We'll have to bring the *Em-Tee* ashore," Mike said.

"And bring in the garden furniture," Tess said.

"And collect candles and flashlights," Mrs. Davis added. "The electric power may fail."

"I almost forgot!" Tess said. "Peter is here!"

She looked at Mike. He looked at her.

"Good morning," Peter said. He stood in the kitchen

doorway. He was still wearing the clothes he had worn when he arrived. "I didn't mean to fall asleep," he said. "I'm sorry."

"It wasn't your fault, Peter," Mrs. Davis said. "You had had a long day—and a long trip. No wonder you were tired! But you must be very hungry now," she added, smiling.

"I am, rather." Suddenly Peter grinned. "Bacon!" he said. "I thought that was what I smelled. How wizard!"

"What does wizard mean?" Tess asked quickly, before she lost her nerve. "Does it mean good?"

"Oh, much better than good!" Peter said. "It means—well, it means smashing."

"And what does smashing mean?" Tess asked.

Peter grinned. "I'm afraid smashing means wizard."

"I see." Tess grinned back at him. She decided she liked Peter after all. She thought he might have a lot of things to say besides wizard and smashing. When they all knew each other better, that is. "So wizard really means terrific," she said. "And smashing means terrific too."

Peter had a question of his own. "Do you always get up this early in America?" he wanted to know.

Mike shook his head. "We're up early because something special is going to happen today. Not something wizard, exactly. But it might turn out to be smashing."

"Mike!" Tess said. "This is no time to be funny. A hurricane is coming, Peter. It's called Audrey."

Peter's eyes got as round as marbles. "You mean a real hurricane is going to strike here? At Southport?"

"I'm afraid so, Peter," Mrs. Davis said.

"A real hurricane!" Peter repeated. "That's—" He

stopped, as if he couldn't find the right word. "But that's absolutely wizard!" he said.

He looked quickly at Mrs. Davis, and then at Tess and at Mike.

"I'm sorry," he said. "Probably a hurricane isn't wizard at all. It's probably rather scary, isn't it? But when you made a joke about it—"

He stopped again, and this time he looked just at Mike. "You did make a joke about it," he said. "You said it was something not wizard, but maybe smashing." Then he smiled, and waited to see if Mike smiled too.

Mike was thinking it wasn't Peter's fault that they couldn't give him a good time, because of the hurricane. It wouldn't be Peter's fault that they wouldn't have a motor for the *Em-Tee* either. And Peter was being a pretty good sport, he thought. Mike did smile, finally.

"It would be scary if we lived on the ocean," he said. He told Peter about the two houses Betsy had smashed. "But back here on Duck Creek we'll probably just have some water on the lawn. Only we can't have the boat picnic we planned for you."

"I've gone on picnics at home," Peter said. "I'd rather see a hurricane any day."

"Sit down, all of you," Mrs. Davis said. "We may not be able to use the electric stove much longer. The power lines may go down. So we'll eat a good hot meal while we can. Do you like your eggs fried, Peter?"

"Yes, please," Peter told her. "Just on one side."

"We call that *sunny side up,*" Tess said.

Peter grinned at her. "So do we," he said.

While they ate, they planned the jobs to be done. Peter asked if he could help. So Mike gave him a pair

27

of jeans and some sneakers. Then they all went to work.

In the garage Mike picked up two long canvas tubes. They looked like limp balloons.

"These are our boat rollers," Mike told Peter. While he blew one of them up, Peter blew up the other.

When the tubes were full of air, they looked like fat sausages. Mike carried one and Peter carried the other. Tess and Mrs. Davis went with them out to the dock.

The wind was already blowing hard. It bent the flowers flat, and tossed the tree branches wildly about. Leaves and twigs sailed through the air.

28

Mike jumped into the *Em-Tee* and untied her. "Pull her around to the beach," he said.

Peter and Mrs. Davis and Tess took hold of the rope. They all pulled. The boat swung around the corner of the dock. When her bow touched land, Mike jumped ashore.

The year before Mike had helped a friend pull his boat out of the water. He remembered what they had done.

"We have to put one roller under her now," he said. He put a blown-up tube close to the *Em-Tee's* bow.

"Come on, Peter," Mike said. "You and I will take this side. Tess, you help Mother."

Eight hands grabbed the *Em-Tee*, four on each side.

"Lift, everybody!" Mike said.

They all lifted at once. The boat's bow rose several inches. Mike kicked the roller under it.

"O.K." Mike said. "Now pull!"

They all dragged at the *Em-Tee*. Her bow moved over the roller. They kept pulling. Finally the roller was beneath the boat's middle seat. The *Em-Tee* balanced on the tube like a see-saw.

"Now another roller," Mike said. He pushed it under the *Em-Tee's* bow, so that she lay on two rollers.

"Forward now," Mike said. "But easy!"

The *Em-Tee* rolled forward on the tubes.

Soon the rear roller was left behind.

"Bring that one up here now," Mike ordered.

Peter understood right away. He picked up the rear roller, ran with it to the front of the boat, and put it under the bow.

29

Once more the boat rolled forward on both tubes. Then it was time to bring the rear one forward again.

Pull. Move a roller. Pull. Move the other roller. Finally they had to stop to catch their breath.

"Where will you leave her?" Peter asked.

"We'll have to put her in the garage," Mike said. "In last year's hurricane, almost the whole lawn was under water."

Peter looked around as if he was trying to imagine water covering all the grass.

"It must have seemed very strange," Peter said.

"But not dangerous," Mrs. Davis told him. "If the water ever got very high, we could climb the hill on the other side of the road, up to the Fosters' house."

"But if the water got that high, it would be in the house!" Peter said. He looked at the one-story Davis cottage.

"You're right, Peter," Mrs. Davis said. "But the water didn't touch the house last year. We hope it never will."

"Ready, everybody?" Mike asked. "Let's go!"

Again they pulled. Peter brought the rear roller forward, and once more they pulled.

There was no entrance on the side of the garage near the water. They had to roll the boat all the way around the building.

Finally they reached the front of the garage. There was room for the *Em-Tee* next to Mrs. Davis's car.

"Once more!" Mike said.

A minute later he said, "She's in!"

They left the *Em-Tee* standing on the two rollers.

30

"Now let's bring in the garden stuff," Tess said.

There were six chairs and a table on the grass near the rose bed. All of them had been blown over.

Tess picked up a chair. She had to hang on to it very tightly. The wind almost blew it out of her hands.

They each carried a chair to the garage. Mrs. Davis stayed there to pile them up. Mike and Peter and Tess went back for the two other chairs and the table.

"There!" Mrs. Davis said. "Now let's close the door."

Afterward, bending against the wind, they ran for the house.

32

They stood in the kitchen, panting.

"Mother!" Tess said suddenly. "The Corrells are away. And the twins' duck is in their back yard!"

"The twins' what?" Mrs. Davis asked.

"Their duck—their plastic raft. It's so light it will float away if water comes onto their lawn," Tess said.

"Oh, dear!" Mrs. Davis said. "We'd better go and get it. Peter," she added, "you could stay here."

"Please, I'd rather help with the raft," Peter said.

Mrs. Davis smiled at him. "Come along then," she said.

The Correll house was a few hundred feet down the road, beyond the little bridge. The stretch of water on the far side of the bridge was Southport Bay. Duck Creek entered the bay right at the bridge.

The wind was behind them. It pushed them along the road, like strong hands shoving at their backs.

At the bridge they stopped, hanging on to the railing.

The tide was coming in fast. It raced beneath their feet, just a foot below the bridge.

Mike shouted over the wind. "If the water's this high, our dock must be covered by now!"

"Hurry!" Mrs. Davis said.

The twins' plastic raft had been blown against the house. It had a duck's head at one end. It looked like a big duck trying to climb the wall.

Mike and Peter pulled it off. The wind almost carried it away. They held it between them, and hung on hard.

They started back.

Now they were facing into the wind. Stinging sand

33

blew into their faces. Mrs. Davis kept her arm around Tess.

This time they didn't pause at the bridge. But they saw that the water had risen several more inches.

The sky was full of black clouds now. It made the day seem dark, as if the sun had set.

They were all glad to be inside the house again.

Mike and Peter dropped the raft.

"Wow!" Mike said.

Peter gasped. Then he said, "Wow!" too.

Mrs. Davis looked through a window facing the creek.

"The water *is* over our dock, Mike," she said. "Even the railing is covered. And the bottom slope of the lawn."

They all went to stand beside her.

Usually Duck Creek was a small stream. Now it looked like a big river. It had overflowed its banks on both sides and covered the lower slopes of the lawns.

Usually the wind made only tiny ruffles on the water's surface. But now there were real waves in the creek.

The waves seemed to grow higher every minute. And the creek grew wider every minute too.

Suddenly a big branch blew past the window.

"Let's get busy," Mrs. Davis said briskly. "Blowing branches may rip down the power lines. Find our flashlights, Mike. And Tess, you look for candles."

Ten minutes later, three flashlights stood on the kitchen table. With them were a dozen candles, some new, some partly burned.

"Now we'll have light tonight, even if the power fails," Mrs. Davis said. "Water is the next thing we need."

"Water?" Peter looked puzzled. "Don't you have enough water?" he asked.

Mrs. Davis laughed. So did Mike and Tess.

"That's salt water," Mike told him, pointing out at the creek. "Mom means water for drinking and stuff. If the power fails, our water pump stops. Then no water comes out of our faucets."

"Oh!" Peter said. "I see."

Mrs. Davis took pots and pans out of the cupboard.

"Fill these," she ordered. "I'll turn on the water in the bathtub. We'll fill that too."

Finally all the pots and pans were full of water. They stood on the stove. They stood on the drainboard. They

stood on the work table.

"Look!" Peter said suddenly. "It's like being on a ship!"

They all joined him at the window. The water had reached the house. Now it was running past, on both sides.

"It's never been this high before," Tess said. She felt a little scared. But she didn't want to say so.

"It *is* like being on a ship," Mike said. "There's water on all sides of us!"

"Not at the front of the house yet," Mrs. Davis said calmly. "What time is high tide today, Mike?"

Mike had to think. "It was high tide at nine yesterday morning. That means it will be high today about ten."

"And it's nine o'clock now," Mrs. Davis said. "So the water will go on rising for another hour. If we—"

The ringing of the telephone interrupted her.

The phone was on the desk in the corner of the living room. Mrs. Davis had to turn on the desk lamp. All the corners of the room were dark.

"Hello," she said. "Oh, hello, darling."

Mike and Tess knew it was their father who was calling.

"Yes, we're all right," Mrs. Davis said. "Yes, the water's almost around the house now. But— Hello?"

She waited a moment. "The line went dead," she said then. "The wires must have blown down somewhere."

Suddenly the desk lamp went out.

"There goes the power line!" Mike said.

"Look!" Tess whispered.

She was pointing toward her feet.

They all bent down to look.

There were little rows of bubbles in the cracks between the floor boards.

Bubble! Bubble! Bubble! Under the roar of the wind they could all hear the tiny noise.

"It's happening," Mrs. Davis said, quietly. "The water is coming up into the house!"

Fish in the
Living Room

For a moment they all went on staring at the rows of bubbles. They could hardly believe their eyes.

Then they all spoke at once.

"The rugs!" Mrs. Davis said. "They'll get soaked!"

"Our shoes on the closet floors!" Tess said.

"The books on the bottom shelf of the bookcase!" Mike said.

"Your sneakers, Mike!" Peter was looking down at his own feet. "I'll take them off!"

"No!" Mrs. Davis told Peter. "They don't matter. Peter, you help me. Mike—you rescue the books. Look after the bedrooms, Tess."

Mrs. Davis and Peter began to roll up the rug in front of the fireplace.

Mike pulled books off the bottom shelf of the bookcase. He piled them on the couch.

Tess ran to her mother's bedroom. She noticed the rug beside the bed. She picked it up and put it on a chair. Then she gathered up all the shoes on the closet floor and tossed them on the bed.

Next she ran to Peter's room. His bag was standing on the floor. She snatched it up and put it on the bed. She put the bedside rug on top of it.

There were no rugs in her bedroom or Mike's. She ran straight for her closet. She scooped up her shoes and threw them on the bed.

She started for Mike's room. Then she remembered the toys in her toy cupboard. She opened its door. She took out everything on the floor level—a forgotten doll, a sewing box, two jars of shells, books, games, a puppet. She threw them all on top of her shoes.

In the hall she ran into Mike.

"My room's done," he said. "The kitchen's next."

The rows of bubbles had run together minutes ago. Now the whole floor was covered with water. It was at least half an inch deep. And it was getting deeper every minute.

Mrs. Davis and Peter were already in the kitchen.

"Look!" Mrs. Davis was pointing to the bottom shelf of the food cupboard. It was only an inch above the floor. The water would reach it soon. And it was crowded with boxes of crackers, cereal, rice and other foods.

40

"There's no place to put them!" Mrs. Davis said.

It was true. Every surface in the kitchen was covered with pots and pans of water.

"The dining room table!" Mike said. "We'll do it like a bucket brigade. You hand things to me, Mom. Peter, you stand over there. I'll hand them to you. And you stand just inside the dining room door, Tess. Peter can reach you—and you can reach the table."

Before he finished speaking, Mrs. Davis handed him four boxes of crackers. Mike handed them to Peter. Peter handed them to Tess. Tess put them on the table.

Next came boxes of cereal. Then boxes of rice and noodles and spaghetti. Then packages of cake mix.

Mrs. Davis snatched the last package just in time. The next moment water lapped over the shelf.

"We made it!" she said. She stood up straight. "But we can't stop for a minute," she went on. "We've rescued only things closest to the floor. Think, everyone! What are the next things in danger?"

"The next shelf right there," Mike said. He pointed to the one just above the empty bottom shelf.

"Bottom bureau drawers!" Tess said.

"Next-to-the-bottom book shelf," Peter said.

They used the brigade system again for the next shelf of food. Then they rushed to the other emergency points.

Tess started for her mother's bedroom. Mrs. Davis followed.

"We won't stop to empty the drawer," Mrs. Davis said. "We'll just take the whole thing out and put it on the bed."

41

It was heavy. They lifted it together.

Next they put Tess's bottom bureau drawer on her bed, and Mike's on his. The beds were getting pretty crowded.

"The linen closet!" Mrs. Davis said suddenly.

She and Tess ran into the hall. The closet's lowest shelf was still above the water. Mrs. Davis handed Tess blankets, two at a time. Tess sloshed into the nearest bedroom. She piled them on the bureau.

Back in the living room, Mike and Peter had cleared the next-to-the-bottom book shelf. Now the whole couch was covered with books.

"The couch cover and the chair covers are getting wet at the bottom," Tess said.

"I know," her mother said. "But we can't pick up the couch."

"We could pick up the chairs though," Peter said. "And put them on top of the books."

So they did. They put three chairs, upside down, on top of the books on top of the couch.

The water was above their ankles now, and rising faster than ever. It was in motion too. At the front of the house, it lapped at the wall with little waves.

"Look!" Peter said suddenly. "They're floating!"

He was pointing to the wooden chairs in the dining room. They were tilted on their sides, riding the surface of the water. They were moving slowly toward the front of the house.

"And look there—and there!" Mike said.

The wooden footstools in the living room were floating too. So was the stool in the kitchen. And the twin's raft. Everything was moving slowly in the same direction.

"They're moving in with the tide!" Mike said.

"Mike's right!" Peter said. "That's what they're doing."

After a minute Tess understood what they meant.

As the tide rose, the whole creek was spreading farther inland. And the water inside the house was part of the creek. It was trying to spread farther inland too. So all the furniture floating in it was being carried to the inland side of the house. It was being carried toward the front walls of the living room and the dining room.

While they watched it, the raft floated through the kitchen door. It floated on toward the dining room table. It got stuck there, between the legs.

Then one of the dining room chairs reached the wall. It stayed there, banging gently with each ripple.

"What should we do next, Mrs. Davis?" Peter asked.

Tess and Mike stopped watching the floating furniture and looked at their mother too.

Mrs. Davis looked at all of them.

"We could leave the house," she said slowly. "We could climb up the hill to the Fosters. They would take us in."

"But we can't leave, Mother!" Tess said. "We have to stay here and take care of things!"

"Sure we do," Mike said. Then he remembered that Peter was their guest. "But if Peter wants to go—" he said.

"Oh, no!" Peter said. "I think we should move the next shelf of things in the kitchen. This very minute. Don't you?"

They thought so too.

"But," said Mrs. Davis, "if the water comes up to the underside of the couch, we'll have to leave." Mike and Tess and Peter all nodded.

By the brigade system they cleared off the third-from-the-bottom kitchen shelf. When they were finished, the dining room table was piled high. Cartons stood on boxes. Cans stood on cartons.

"It's a good thing we've put so much on it," Peter said. "Now the table can't float."

Then they took out all the next-to-the-bottom bureau drawers. When they were finished, every bed was piled high too.

Finally they moved another whole shelf of books. They piled them on the bottoms of the chairs—the

45

chairs that were piled on the books that were piled on the couch.

By now the water reached Tess's knees. It was almost touching the bottom of the mattresses on the beds. It was almost touching the underside of the couch.

"If it comes up one more inch—" Mrs. Davis said.

Tess broke in, too excited to let her mother finish. "Everything's floating the other way now! Look!"

"It is! It is!" Mike shouted.

The dining room chairs were no longer banging against the front wall. Now they were moving back, slowly, toward the table. The duck-headed raft was heading for the kitchen. The kitchen stool was drifting back toward the work table. The footstools were moving back toward the bookcase.

"The tide has turned!" Mike said.

"Thank heaven!" Mrs. Davis smiled.

Looking at her, Tess and Mike knew for the first time how worried she had been.

"Now the water will start to go down," Mrs. Davis said. "The wind is dying down too," she added. "Listen."

Standing knee deep in water, they all listened.

The roar of the wind was certainly not as loud as it had been earlier.

Just then a knock sounded on the front door.

Everybody looked toward it, startled.

"Do people in America go visiting in the middle of a hurricane?" Peter asked.

They stared at him for a second. Then they all burst out laughing.

46

They were still laughing as they waded to the door. Mike opened it.

In poured a rush of soggy leaves, twigs and other small things. And in came Mr. and Mrs. Correll. Mrs. Correll carried Jody in her arms. Mr. Correll carried Jim.

"Hi, Tess!" Jody shouted. "Do you know this is a hurry-up-cane?"

"Mrs. Davis," Mrs. Correll said, "we hate to do this to you. But we have been trying to get back to our own house. And we can't cross the bridge. It's under water."

"May we stay an hour or so?" Mr. Correll asked. "The tide has turned now. The water should go down as fast as it came up."

"I want to swim!" Jim said. "I want to swim with the fishes!"

"Me too, Mommy!" Jody said. "I want to swim with the fishes, too."

He was pointing at the water.

Then everybody else saw them—the tiny minnows darting around the flooded room. They swam under the couch and out again. They nosed against desk legs and people's legs.

"Fish in the living room!" Peter said. "It's the most wizard thing I ever saw in my whole life!"

"Down, Mommy!" Jody begged.

"Down, Daddy! Down, Daddy!" Jim echoed.

They made a lot of noise when they both yelled at once.

Mrs. Correll looked at Mrs. Davis. "I don't mind

them getting wet," she said. "It's so warm it can't hurt them. But you don't want them splashing about the house."

"I know!" Tess said. "They can sit in their raft!"

She and Mike and Peter brought it in from the kitchen.

"Our duck! Our duck!" Jim and Jody shouted.

Mrs. Davis told Mrs. Correll how they had rescued it. Mr. Correll put the twins in the raft. He told them to stay there.

"I'll look after them," Tess said.

"We'll help. Won't we, Mike?" Peter said.

"Let's see what we can find for lunch," Mrs. Davis said. The Corrells went with her to the kitchen.

Soon Mrs. Davis called, "Come, children."

Tess and Peter pulled the twins' raft with them. Mrs. Davis had cleared one corner of the dining room table. Plates and bowls of food were piled on that corner.

"The chairs don't float if you sit on them," Mr. Correll said. He set a chair upright for Tess, and held it for her. They all sat down. The duck raft floated beside the table.

They ate cheese and ham sandwiches. They ate two kinds of pickles and two kinds of potato chips.

"This is what we planned to eat on our boat picnic today," Tess told Peter.

He grinned. "They taste good at a hurricane picnic too. Everything is wizard."

"Are you sure it's not smashing?" Tess asked, smiling.

"What's wizard mean?" Jody asked.

"What's smashing mean?" Jim asked.

Mike kept a straight face. "Wizard means smashing," he said. "And smashing means wizard."

"And they both mean terrific!" Peter said.

Then he and Tess and Mike all laughed. They felt as if they had been friends for years.

While they ate, the water went down—and down—and down. The twins' raft sank closer and closer to the floor.

After a time the water came only to Tess's ankles. When they finished eating, it was only an inch deep.

"Come!" Mrs. Davis said. "We'll get brooms and sweep the rest right out the door!"

They all went to the front door and opened it. The gray clouds were disappearing. The sun was shining through. The wind had died down to a tiny breeze.

The hurricane was over.

Mrs. Davis looked around at the soggy dead leaves and twigs everywhere. She looked at the wet skirt of the couch cover. "What a mess!" Then she smiled. "But nothing is really ruined. I don't believe we've lost a single thing!"

"We lost our fishes!" Jody said.

"Yes, we did," Jim said. "We lost all our fishes!"

"Come on," Tess said to them. "Maybe we can find some that got caught in the grass. Let's look." Then she said quietly to Mrs. Correll, "I'll take care of them." It wasn't safe to leave the twins alone with the back lawn still flooded.

"Thank you," Mrs. Correll said. "Then Mr. Correll and I can help your mother clean up. She wouldn't have all those twigs and things in the house if you hadn't opened the door to us."

Mike and Peter joined the clean-up squad too.

They were still working hard when a taxi stopped in front of the house. Mr. Davis and another man got out.

"Daddy!" Tess ran to her father.

Peter was wringing out a mop near the front door.

"Father!" he said suddenly. And he ran to the second man.

Mrs. Davis and Mike and the Corrells came out. Everyone talked at once.

Tess and Mike and Peter told how the water had come into the house. They told how they had rescued things.

The two men told their story too.

Mr. Blake said he had called Mr. Davis when he heard about Audrey. Mr. Davis had explained to him about the dead telephone line. They had agreed to go to the Davis cottage together.

But their train was halted halfway to Southport. The hurricane had flooded the tracks. The train had to wait until the water went down. Then it had started again.

"So everything is all right at last," Mr. Davis said. "We finally got here. And we find you all safe and sound."

"They even saved the twins' raft," Mr. Correll said. And he told about that.

Then the Corrells said the bridge was surely above water now. They put the twins and their raft in the car, and drove away. Jim and Jody waved. Tess and Mike and Peter waved back.

"Those twins are very clever for four-year-olds," Peter said.

"Yes, they are," Tess said. She was glad Peter thought so too. It made her like him more than ever.

"Let's see where the water is now," Mr. Davis said.

52

They all walked around to the other side of the house. The lowest part of the lawn was still flooded. But already the top railing of the dock was showing.

"I don't see the *Em-Tee!*" Mr. Davis said. "She must have been carried away."

"Oh, no!" Mike and Tess and Peter all spoke together. Then they told him how they had rolled the boat into the garage.

"Good for you!" Mr. Davis said. "I'm proud of you— all of you!"

"That's a strange name for a boat," Mr. Blake said.

"*Em* stands for M, for Mike," Tess told him.

"And *Tee* stands for T, for Tess," Mike said.

Tess and Mike didn't look at each other. They were glad, now, that Tess's idea hadn't worked. Even if they had given Peter a good visit, it wouldn't seem right to take a gift for it. Not now, knowing Peter the way they did.

"But *Em-Tee* also stands for Empty," Peter said. "It means Empty-because-she-doesn't-have-a-motor-in-her."

Tess and Mike just stared at him. They could feel their faces getting red.

Peter grinned. "Jody and Jim explained it to me," he said. "I told you those twins are clever."

Mr. Davis laughed. He put one arm around Tess, and one arm around Mike. "Cheer up," he said. "By next summer the *Em-Tee* probably won't be empty any more. I'm pretty sure we'll be able to get a motor for her by then."

"Now here's a strange coincidence!" Mr. Blake said suddenly. "You have a boat without a motor. And I have a motor I want to get rid of. Why not put my motor in the *Em-Tee?*"

Mike and Tess stood perfectly still. They couldn't take their eyes off Mr. Blake's face.

"But why should you want to get rid of a motor?" Mr. Davis asked.

"I brought it over here to use as a sample," Mr. Blake explained. "I hope to be selling my products in the United States in the future. And now I'm finished with it."

"But you can take it home with you," Mr. Davis said.

Mike held his breath. So did Tess.

"Yes, I could," Mr. Blake agreed. "But it would cost more to pack it and ship it than the motor is worth.

It's not a big one," he added. "And perhaps if you use it, you would tell me how you like it. You would be doing me a great favor, if you would."

"You mean we could test it for you in American waters?" Mr. Davis was smiling.

"Exactly," Mr. Blake said. He was smiling too. Then he looked at Tess and Mike. "What do you say?" he asked. "Would you be willing to test a Blake Marine Engine for me, in your American creek?"

Mike gulped. He swallowed. He couldn't say a word.

Tess gulped too. "Oh, yes!" she said. "And I have a wonderful idea! Now *Em* can stand for Motor. And *Tee* can stand for Tester. We can tell people the name of our boat means Motor Tester!"

"That's a wizard idea!" Peter said.

"Splendid!" Mr. Blake said. "It's all arranged then. The motor will be delivered to you next week."

Supper that night was a cook-in. Peter and his father both liked the hamburgers. They liked Tess's cake too.

Afterward Tess and Mike carried the dishes out to the kitchen.

"Tess," Mike said, "let's buy Peter a present. Guests should have presents sometimes too, I think."

"Oh, Mike, yes! Let's!" Tess said. "And isn't it a wizard coincidence? We want to buy a present, and we have some money to buy it with. What shall we get?"

"I don't know," Mike said. "We'll have to think about it. But let's get something smashing."

"Yes," Tess said. "Let's!"

They went back into the living room. The fire was blazing.

The room looked gay and bright, lit with many candles.

At just that moment the desk lamp turned on by itself.

The electric power was back.

"You know," Peter said, "this has been the most absolutely terrific day of my whole life!"

"Mine too," Tess said.

And Mike said, "Mine too."